Belfry Bat
the Scaredy Cat

by Gayle McGuire Tremblay

Illustrations by Chum McLeod

SECOND STORY Press

Belfry Bat was scared of mice. She was scared of the moon. And she was terrified of spiders. Just the thought of one made the hair stand straight up on her little brown head! When the wind whistled through the lonely dark attic where she lived with ninety-nine other brown bats, she hid under her wing, quivering with fright.

Sometimes Belfry's little friends were mean to her. They wouldn't play with her because she was no fun at all. They teased her and chanted "Belfry Bat the Scaredy Cat," over and over again. Then they would stick their tongues out at her and fly away through the window, leaving her all alone to shiver and shake in the dark until they came home again.

Belfry and her friends didn't live in just any old attic. They were the luckiest bats in town, because their attic belonged to Mildred — the fastest witch who ever lived.

Mildred could zip over rooftops faster than a speeding rocket. She whizzed above treetops fast enough to scare the birds right out of their nests. She loved to zoom to the airport and then take off faster than the jets. Mildred could race anything!

Well, almost anything. Mildred had never been quite brave enough to race against THUNDER MONSTER, the fastest roller coaster in the whole wide world!

Mildred had been putting it off for weeks. What if she lost? It would be a disaster!

But whoever could she find to help her?

Just then Mildred had a wonderful idea. Wasn't her attic full of little brown bats? And weren't bats amazing creatures with special radar so they never bumped into a single thing? Maybe one of the bats could help her!

Mildred zoomed up the stairs. She looked all around, but there wasn't a single bat to be seen.

Suddenly, Mildred heard a tiny squeak. She turned around, and there was Belfry, hanging upside down all by herself. Mildred was delighted!

Would Belfry *please* sit on the front of her broom and use her special radar power? Would Belfry *please* help her win the race with THUNDER MONSTER?

Belfry couldn't believe her ears! Was the famous Mildred really asking her for help? Belfry squeaked for joy, nodding her head up and down and flapping her little wings.

"Belfry!" Mildred said. "I knew I could count on you. I'll be back to pick you up at nine o'clock."

But Mildred didn't know Belfry's deep dark secret: Belfry was terrified of flying! Just the thought of it made her sick. She had been so excited when the famous Mildred asked for her help she just couldn't keep from nodding her head up and down. What had she been thinking? Didn't she know Mildred was a reckless speed demon? Didn't she know Mildred was faster than a speeding rocket?

That night just before nine o'clock all the bats came flying home. They sneered at Belfry who was hanging there, shivering and shaking. Oh, how Belfry wished her friends wouldn't tease her. Oh, how she wished she wasn't scared of her own shadow!

Suddenly the door crashed open — and there stood the famous Mildred. What was she doing here in the lonely dark attic? The bats almost fainted from happiness.

Then something amazing happened. The mighty Mildred called out Belfry's name! The bats gasped with shock as Belfry fluttered down and perched shakily on Mildred's broom. In a cloud of dust, Mildred and Belfry shot through the window.

Belfry's friends were flabbergasted! Why had Mildred chosen Belfry and not one of them? Didn't Mildred know Belfry was terrified of flying? Didn't Mildred know about Belfry Bat the Scaredy Cat?

Belfry's friends decided to follow. They knew Mildred had picked the wrong bat. They knew Belfry always got sick to her stomach when she was nervous. They wanted to tease Belfry when she threw up and fell off Mildred's broom. They wanted to laugh at her when she landed upside down in someone's garbage can. Belfry Bat wasn't going to get away with this!

Belfry opened her eyes. Mildred really was having the time of her life, swooping and twisting and diving and climbing. She shrieked with joy even as they came to RATTLESNAKE TWIST — a scary, triple loop, and the fastest part of the ride. Belfry wrapped her little claws around the broomstick and moaned.

"Oh, Belfry," shouted Mildred above the sound of the wind. "You're doing such a great job leading the way."

They zipped around the first loop. Belfry held her breath and stole a backward glance at Mildred. She couldn't believe her eyes! Mildred was riding with no hands around RATTLESNAKE TWIST! Belfry could feel her stomach doing flip-flops as she buried her little head under her wing.

Just as Mildred whizzed past the finish line and slammed on the brakes, Belfry peeked out. THUNDER MONSTER was nowhere in sight. Mildred had won the race!

"Belfry, this is the happiest day of my life," Mildred exclaimed as she and Belfry shot off into the clear night sky. "And I owe it all to you. If you hadn't been so brave and led the way, I never would have been able to race THUNDER MONSTER. You are the best bat in the whole world."

Belfry looked out the corner of her eye. She could see all her little friends following close behind. She began to grin. She turned around and looked at Mildred, who had thrown back her head and was laughing with joy.

Belfry Bat sat up tall and proud on the front of the broomstick. Her heart fluttered happily as Mildred soared and swooped high above the treetops. And then, with Belfry leading the way, Mildred headed home.